Challenge
of the
Dragon

Written by
JOAN & DAVID MERKIN
Illustrated by Phil Gerard Godin

Order this book online at www.trafford.com
or email orders@trafford.com

Most Trafford titles are also available at major online book retailers.

Print information available on the last page.

ISBN: 978-1-4907-8311-6 (*sc*)
ISBN: 978-1-4907-8310-9 (*e*)

Library of Congress Control Number: 2017909582

Our mission is to efficiently provide the world's finest, most comprehensive book publishing service, enabling every author to experience
success. To find out how to publish your book, your way, and have it available worldwide, visit us online at www.trafford.com

Any people depicted in stock imagery provided by Thinkstock are models,
and such images are being used for illustrative purposes only.
Certain stock imagery © Thinkstock.

Trafford rev. 06/27/2017

www.trafford.com

North America & international
toll-free: 1 888 232 4444 (USA & Canada)
phone: 250 383 6864 • fax: 812 355 4082

Challenge of the Dragon

by

Joan S. Merkin

and

David B. Merkin

Long, long ago, when magic ruled the Earth and wizards and dragons roamed the land, there was a kingdom called Alestria. Alestria was a beautiful kingdom of rolling hills and majestic mountains, lush green valleys and fertile farmland, crystal clear lakes and streams, and deep green forests. In the center of Alestria stood the king's castle, which was as shiny as gold; it was so bright that it could be seen for miles. The people of Alestria were warm and friendly, and they were blessed with a wise and benevolent king.

The king's name was Vladimir. He was an old man who stood about six feet tall, with a pale complexion and graying black hair and a beard to match. King Vladimir had two children, the twins Prince Valerian and Princess Alisia. The prince was just a little taller than his father, but he was as brave as a lion, sly as a fox, and very handsome with his blue eyes and strong body. The princess was slender and beautiful, and wherever she went, the sun would shine and the birds would begin to sing, and all the boys of the kingdom wished that she would look their way. Clearly, the king's wife, Queen Rena, had passed her beauty down to her daughter. But Alisia had also inherited her mother's legendary grace and intelligence. And to both her children she passed on a special gift, for the queen was a very powerful sorceress, and the children shared in their mother's power.

Before her death, she called for her children, who were eight at the time, to impart her wisdom to them before she died. After she taught them as much as she could in the time she had left, she said to them, "My children, you must always take care of each other, for though you both have the knowledge of magic and sorcery, only when you work together will you never be defeated." Then she opened a little box and took out the contents from within.

In her hand, she held two golden rings; each had a ruby stone in the middle of it, and on the inside of each band was written a word. Then the queen gave one ring to each of the twins. "These rings will enable you to take on any shape or form," the queen said. "All you need to do is say the magic word written on your ring and think of the shape you wish to assume. It will also give you many other powers. Use them wisely." Her final words to them were "only use your powers for good and never evil." Then her eyes closed, and she was gone.

A few years had passed since their mother's death. Both the prince and princess were now almost in their teenage years. One day, a mysterious black cloud came over the sky and covered the kingdom. The longer the cloud was there, the more it seemed as if Alestria was dying under its presence. The crops weren't growing, the people were suffering and the land was plagued with disease. Nothing could be done. Finally, King Vladimir called for his children. When they appeared before him, he said, "My children, our kingdom's only hope is you, but I fear that I may never see you again."

Just then, Prince Valerian told his father that he and Alisia would save the kingdom and that they would return to him. Prince Valerian and Princess Alisia quickly made their preparations for their quest, and they set off the next morning.

As they left the gates of the castle, their father turned to them and said, "Goodbye, my children. Be well and safe, and return home as soon as you can." Then he added, "I love you."

For companions, they had their horses, Pearl and Myjestyx, and their longtime friend and playmate, Shirekan the tiger. As they traveled through Alestria, the whole kingdom came to say goodbye and wish them good luck, for they too knew that their only chance of survival rested with the prince and princess. As they reached the border of Alestria, they turned and took one last look at their beloved kingdom. Then turning their mounts toward the east and an uncertain future that awaited them, they continued on their way.

They decided to head for the one place where they knew they would find the cause of this terrible cloud—the kingdom of Darkoria. Darkoria was a three-day journey from Alestria. It was a dark and foreboding realm ruled by Terresca, the most powerful dragon in all the land. They knew that Terresca reserved his deepest hatred for Alestria and King Vladimir. Many was the time they had sat enraptured as the minstrels would recount the story of how Terresca was banished to Darkoria by the king and queen many years before.

At the time, Terresca roamed throughout the kingdoms of the west, striking fear into all the inhabitants as he ravaged their kingdoms. All who had tried to stop him failed, and Terresca and his henchman ruled the ravaged countryside. Soon their reign of terror had reached the borders of Alestria. Determined to save Alestria, a young Prince Vladimir went to his father and asked to leave to go lead an army to challenge the dragon. With his father's blessing, Vladimir led his forces in the direction that the latest messengers had brought word of Terresca's whereabouts. Meanwhile, another stranger had entered the borders of Alestria. She was a beautiful young sorceress named Rena, who had sworn vengeance upon Terresca for killing her beloved mentor. After many months of tracking the dragon and battles with those he had sent to stop her, she had finally drawn close to him. Now she was determined that none would stand between her and him. While traveling along the roads of Alestria, she came upon the encampment of a great army. Deducing that the army was on its way to battle Terresca, she decided to seek out the army's commander and offer her aid to him. She was presented to Prince Vladimir and his generals.

To these assembled warriors she said, "I am Rena the sorceress, sworn enemy of Terresca. After many hardships, I have caught up with him. I presume that you too are seeking him out? I offer my services to you, and perhaps together, we can rid the lands of this terrible scourge."

Vladimir stepped forward. This was the most beautiful woman he had ever seen; and as she spoke, he felt himself falling in love with her. He swore he would make her his bride one day.

But getting back to the matter at hand, he said, "I am Vladimir, Prince of Alestria. And you are correct. We are on our way to stop Terresca. On behalf of myself and my men, I accept you offer, for surely, the presence of a talented sorceress would benefit our cause greatly."

As the army took off for their battle, Rena noticed this funny feeling she had never felt before when looking at the prince. "Perhaps," she thought, "could I be falling in love?"

After a couple of days, the army caught up with Terresca and his army on a great plain near the village of Mirmey Way. As the two forces took to the battlefield, Vladimir said to Rena, "Stay by my side. For if it is Terresca's head you value, I will help you achieve it."

As the trumpets signaled the start of the battle, the two forces clashed with a great roar as men, goblins, and trolls crossed swords with the future of Alestria at stake. As the number of dead grew, Terresca's army started to give ground; at this point, he waded into the battle himself with his bodyguard. This was the moment that Vladimir had been waiting for. With his own bodyguard, and Rena, he charged into the thick of battle, right for Terresca. Soon they had cut through the enemy to Terresca himself.

As the two groups of bodyguards clashed, Terresca faced Vladimir and Rena alone. With the first strike of his sword, Vladimir nipped Terresca's leg, causing the dragon to let out a shriek of pain. But lest any be fooled as to Terresca's strength, he fought back savagely with fire, tooth, and claw, as Vladimir charged with his sword while Rena used lightning bolts and fireballs upon him. Finally, exhausted and bleeding from many wounds, Terresca fell to the ground, defeated. At this point, what was left of his army fell apart, and was scattered to the four corners of the map by Vladimir's victorious forces.

Rena now moved toward Terresca and readied a lightning bolt to strike through his heart and send the vile beast to oblivion. Just then, a voice from behind told her to stop. She and Vladimir and those nearby turned to see an image in the sky, and a startled Rena whispered, "Mordimar!" Truly, there was the face of Rena's beloved mentor, the great wizard Mordimar.

Mordimar said to her, "My child, enough blood has been shed today already. Killing Terresca will not bring me or all those who died during his reign of terror back. Better to banish him beyond the mountains to the lands of the east, where he can do no harm and will be tormented by his failure for the rest of his life."

Swayed by Mordimar's words, Rena and Vladimir agreed to spare Terresca. And so the dragon was dragged in chains to the great mountains that separated the kingdoms of the west from the eastern lands. There, Vladimir, in the name of the western kings, pronounced

Terresca's punishment as eternal banishment and sent him off into exile. As the great beast flew away over the mountains, some said they could see a sinister smile cross his grim face for just a moment. Days later, after much feasting and rejoicing, Rena and Vladimir were married.

With this history in mind, Valerian and Alisia knew that Terresca was probably up to his old evil tricks once more. And so they traveled on, wondering what perils Terresca would have in store for them. They had traveled for many hours and were starting to get sleepy, so they decided to rest and continue in the morning. Just as they began to drift off to sleep, an image appeared before them. It was an image of their mother.

The image started to speak. "BEWARE THE PATH THAT LOOKS FRIENDLY!" And then it was gone.

The prince and princess looked at each other but could not figure out what the cryptic message meant. Soon they drifted off to sleep once more. The next morning, they were roused from their sleep by the loud roar that Shirekan let out. They jumped to their feet to see what it was, but they could see nothing, except that the mysterious cloud had gotten bigger; it seemed as if it was following them. This made them more determined than ever to continue on their quest. As they traveled, Princess Alisia turned to her brother.

"Valerian," she asked, "do you remember what Mother told us about Terresca?"

"Vaguely," Valerian replied.

Alisia continued, "Terresca's mentor was Mordimar, the most powerful wizard of all. He had found Terresca when he was small and took him under his wing, taught Terresca everything he knew about magic and sorcery. But as Terresca grew, Mordimar found that all he used his magic for was evil. Mordimar could not stand for it, but Terresca was already more powerful than him. And so Mordimar died trying to stop Terresca." Alisia then added, "Valerian, my brother, we must be careful. Terresca will be our greatest challenge, and we must not fail, for our kingdom depends on us."

Suddenly, Valerian said, "Alisia, look."

They had come upon a fork in the road and had to make a decision whether to take the left path or the right. The path to the left was overgrown and rutted, and at points, it seemed to be swallowed up by the forest. The right path was well-worn and was as straight and level as an arrow.

Valerian turned to Alisia and said, "The image told us to beware the path that looks friendly. That could mean the path that looks more traveled."

Alisia agreed, so they took the left path, which had hardly been traveled at all. After traveling for many hours, they decided to get some sleep; and again, the image appeared.

This time, the image warned, "TO DEFEAT YOUR ENEMY, YOU MUST STRIKE AT THAT WHICH IS EMPTY." And then it vanished.

Alisia and Valerian again could not figure out the message, so they went to sleep. Shirekan again awoke them the next morning with a loud roar, but again they saw nothing except that the cloud had grown even bigger.

Prince Valerian and Princess Alisia started on their journey again, but after a few hours of traveling, they saw what they had traveled all this way for. They had come to the stone arch that marked the gateway to Darkoria. As they looked through the gateway, they could see in the distance the large claw-shaped tower that was home to Terresca. And they knew the time was coming when they must meet their great enemy for the sake of their kingdom.

With a shudder, they quickly turned their gaze from the tower. Looking at the kingdom stretched out below them, they could see that Darkoria was as dark as the midnight sky. Just looking at that dark kingdom could scare anyone. The fields and forests and even the rivers were as black as a witch's heart! Even the towns were black, and the only light was the red light of the inhabitants' fires. It was rumored that the kingdom was crawling with goblins, trolls, witches, and other evil creatures. As they looked through the gate, down the path before them, they saw it meander down to the valley floor, where it marched straight to the edge of the forest below and disappeared into the surrounding gloom.

Before going any further, Valerian said the magic word "ARCON," and his ring began to glow a bright yellow.

Then he said "Form of an owl," and suddenly, a great owl appeared where Valerian had just stood a moment before. He took flight to scout up ahead to make sure it was safe and to look for any immediate dangers that they should be aware of.

After a thorough look, Valerian flew back and changed into himself almost as fast as he changed into the owl. Not seeing any immediate danger, Valerian and Alisia mounted their horses and cautiously continued down the path with Shirekan leading them as a lookout for dangers not seen. When they reached the edge of the forest, they stopped for a moment. Looking down the path, they could see that after a few feet, it was too dark to see inside the forest.

Valerian turned to his sister and said, "It would appear that we will need some light to continue on our journey. Any suggestions?"

"Just one," Alisia responded.

Thereupon, she held out her hand, palm facing the sky, and said a magic spell. Her hand then filled with a bright ball of glowing light that grew as big as a melon. Then she added another magic spell, and the ball of light floated ever so gently out of her hand and hovered a couple of feet above their heads.

Now, the area around them for twenty feet in every direction was bathed in the soft glowing light of the ball. With the illumination of the ball, they were now able to see the path through the forest, and so their quest continued. Though surrounded by the pervasive dark of Darkoria outside their field of light, their journey was relatively easy. They saw little of Darkoria's evil inhabitants. Those that did try to attack them were easily dealt with by Shirekan or a useful magic spell. So, they found their journey to be moving along rather quickly.

As they neared Terresca's tower, they noticed how gloomy it was, and that it was surrounded by a constant cloud of thunder and lightning. The tower stood upon a rocky hill, which was circled by a road that wound up the hill to the tower's black gate. Turning off the path before it joined the main road to the tower, they found a small glen near the foot of the hill. Dismounting from their horses, they decided to leave Pearl and Myjestyx hidden in the glen for safety. As an added measure of protection, Valerian cast an invisibility spell over their faithful horses.

Continuing on foot, the pair, accompanied by Shirekan, started to climb the hill. When they neared the gate, they noticed it was heavily guarded by goblins and trolls; but as luck should have it, a column of goblins was marching toward the front gate. So both Valerian and Alisia said their respective magic words—"ARCON" and "NOCRA"—and took the forms of goblins. As for Shirekan, Alisia cast a spell on him that made him appear as a wolf. Joining the rear of the column as it passed their hiding place, they marched with the column through the gates and into the tower with Shirekan by their side. They thought they were undetected when they jumped into a hall to hide and wait, but far up in the darkest and scariest part of the castle, Terresca was looking at what appeared to be a mirror, and in it, he could see Valerian and Alisia entering his castle.

He stood up and said to his faithful servant Bablo, "Now the game begins." And he let out a loud and sinister laugh.

In the meantime, after the goblins were gone, Valerian and Alisia changed back into their own forms. They then turned towards Shirekan. Raising their arms in his direction, they touched their rings together and said their magic words "ARCON" and "NOCRA" at the same time and turned Shirekan from the faithful companion and guardian into a huge battle cat with armor, whose roar was so ferocious that it would make a goblin or troll run with the first roar he let out.

The three of them continued down the hall carefully so as not to be seen by anyone. Soon they came to a great huge door that had bolts all over it and a lock with no key to be seen anywhere. When they looked through the door's barred window, they saw an old man, with a long white beard. He seemed to be of average height. He was very thin and was as white as a ghost. They thought he looked familiar to them, but were unable to place him.

Alisia said to Valerian, "The only way to get to him is through the door, and to get through the door, we need a key. Any ideas?"

"Just one," Valerian said. And he added, "If you want a key, you have to use your head and make one, or use the wonderful magic that we have learned."

Then Alisia said, "And which would you prefer—magic or making a key?"

Valerian then said, "Magic is always nice, quiet, and fun." Then he said the following spell:

"The door is barred and we have no key, but for keys I have no need.
 For with a word at lightning speed, the lock will open up for me."

Suddenly, the lock opened with a click, and Alisia removed the lock and opened the door.

Leaving Shirekan to guard the door, they walked inside. They crossed over to the old man, who jumped with surprise when Alisia softly touched him.

Alisia said to him, "I am Princess Alisia, and this is my brother, Prince Valerian. We are from the kingdom—"

Before Alisia could finish, the old man replied in a weak and shaky voice, "I know who you are, for your mother, Queen Rena, was one of my apprentices. And you, Princess Alisia, are as beautiful and mystifying as she was."

Because Valerian did not like that this old man knew who they were and they knew nothing of him, he snapped, "And who might you be, old man?"

The old man replied, "I am Mordimar, the most powerful wizard in all the world."

"But how can this be?" Alisia said. "Our mother told us you died trying to stop Terresca."

"That was what Terresca wanted everyone to think," the old man replied, "so that all would fear his so-called power. But while we were battling, his guards grabbed me from behind and took me prisoner. He entrusted me to his servant Bablo and told him to take me to Darkoria for safekeeping while he attacked the western kingdoms. However, I had hoped that I would be rescued after Terresca lost to you parents;. But he tricked everyone by using the magic I had taught him to make an image of me appear and save his own vile skin and, in the process, leaving everyone to continue believing that I was dead. After he came to Darkoria, Terresca built this tower and threw me in this room to die."

The wizard then added, "Children, together you can defeat Terresca. It will be difficult, but your powers together are more than a match for him."

"Then," Valerian said, "together we shall finish the job our parents started and destroy this cursed beast to save our world."

The old man pointed to a torch on the far wall and said, "My children, that torch opens a secret door that leads straight to Terresca's lair. But be careful not to look Terresca in the eyes, for he is a master of hypnotism."

Alisia went to get Shirekan while Valerian pulled on the torch. The secret door opened, and the three started though it.

Alisia turned to Mordimar and said, "We shall return for you."

After a few minutes of walking, they came to the end of the hall. There was a wooden ladder that led up to what appeared to be a trapdoor. Alisia climbed up to take a look. She lifted the door ever so slightly so as not to attract attention. Then in the corner of the room, she saw him. It was Terresca. He was fifteen feet high, with dry rough scales and a grey-black color, and he was as mean-looking as a pack of hungry alligators. Alisia slowly shut the door and quietly climbed back down the ladder. Turning to Valerian, she began to tell him what she had seen in the room above.

"There are five guards with him—three goblins and two trolls."

Valerian thought for a moment then said, "We can take the form of a goblin or troll and stroll right into his lair. Then when they don't expect it, we attack." Alisia, although not entirely convinced that the plan would work, agreed to go along with it. So she turned into a goblin and Valerian turned into a troll, and up the ladder they went, leaving Shirekan to wait for their call.

When they got to Terresca's chamber, they were very quiet so as not to call attention to themselves. Then they waited, and when all those present in the chamber were not looking in their direction, they crept out from the trapdoor into the chamber. Taking places in the corner of the room, they observed what was happening. They were relieved to see that Terresca's minions were coming and going from room to room with regularity, so the sudden appearance of two new "guards" would not cause alarm. Terresca was pacing back and forth in front of a mirror on the other side of the room. He seemed quite angry, and those around him looked concerned, lest he take his anger out on them.

All the while, Terresca kept screaming, "Why have I lost the picture? What happened to my magic mirror? One moment, I am watching the two little brats with the old wizard, and the next, nothing."

Valerian turned to Alisia and said, "I think he's talking about us."

"Yes," Alisia replied. "It is a good thing he did not see us coming through the secret passageway or we might be dead right now. I wonder if Mordimar had something to do with it."

Valerian smiled and said, "Who else? But I'm surprised the old man still has it in him. After all, if he could use his magic, why didn't he escape before?"

The question puzzled the two of them, but they knew that the answer would have to wait until they met Mordimar again.

Valerian and Alisia now wondered what their next move would be. Clearly, they must eliminate the guards before confronting Terresca —but how? A few moments passed, when, suddenly, a guard burst through the door.

"My Lord," he said excitedly, "the twins have been spotted in the fifth level, near the armory."

With this news, Valerian and Alisia exchanged a puzzled look.

"Excellent," Terresca said with a sinister gleam in his eyes. "Now I have them." Terresca then ordered that all available troops in the tower be sent to the fifth level in hopes of trapping Valerian and Alisia.

As the door closed behind the last of the guards to leave the chamber Terresca called out, "Be sure not to hurt them. I want that pleasure for myself."

At this point, the chamber was nearly empty. Only Terresca, Bablo, and a handful of guards remained. Valerian and Alisia knew that now was the time to strike. In hushed tones, they made up a plan of action, and they carefully left their corner and walked through the door. Neither Terresca nor his guards seemed to notice their movement. Upon reaching the door, Alisia went to the lock and bolted it while Valerian stood in front of her to block her actions from sight. For good measure, Alisia cast a spell that fused the lock.

"There," she whispered, "no one will be getting in or out of this room now."

Joining her brother, the two looked around the room. Terresca and Bablo were busy with the magic mirror. Terresca kept trying to get it to work since he didn't want to miss the capture of Valerian and Alisia. The guards were standing in various places around the room, forming a loose defensive ring around Terresca. Feeling no immediate danger to their lord, they seemed not to be paying attention to what was going on.

"It seems," Valerian said, "that the old lizard is so interested in seeing our capture that we shall get him and his guards with the same spell."

Alisia nodded in agreement.

Wasting not a moment more, Valerian and Alisia returned to their human forms and began to cast a magic spell:

"Of flesh and blood and bone, these evil creatures were born. But for them evil will soon mourn, as with our spell they turn to stone."

Finishing the magic words, the twins paused a moment, and said to Terresca, "Looking for us, lizard face?"

Startled, Terresca and his henchmen turned to see Valerian and Alisia standing there. But before they could move a step, the twins raised their arms over their heads, and out of their hands shot beams of light. One by one, the guards turned to stone as they were hit by a beam. Terresca, being more cleaver than his henchmen, spread his wings and flew out of the way of the beam. Missing Terresca, the beam hits the magic mirror, turning it to stone—whereupon the mirror shattered into a million pieces. By this time, the beams had stopped shooting around the room, and all was quiet. Terresca, hovering above the room, viewed the damage that had been done. There he saw the pieces of his once beloved magic mirror and six stone statues that looked like his loyal guards and faithful servant.

Just then, Terresca said, "You fools, you are no match for me. I will avenge this outrage, for this shall be the day when you join your mother again."

Valerian then said, "No, Terresca, for we shall be your undoing." And with that, he threw a ball of fire at the dragon.

Without thinking, Terresca spat a stream of fire at the fireball, causing the two to join and disappear in a flash. Alisia then counterattacked with a spear of ice. Being occupied with Valerian's attack, Terresca did not notice Alisia's attack until it was too late. The spear buried itself deep in his left wing, causing him to let out a haunting cry of pain as he plunged to the floor.

Alisia then said, "So it seems the mighty have fallen."

"It looks like the odds have been evened," Valerian added.

"You children," Terresca said as he hurled a lightning bolt and balls of fire at them.

Alisia, thinking fast, created a magic shield between Terresca's attacks and herself and Valerian just seconds before the fireballs strike the shield, creating a fireworks display. However, the blow to the shield was so powerful it knocked them to the floor. Just then, Shirekan burst through the trapdoor. Quickly sizing up the situation, the huge cat leapt at Terresca. Knocking him over, Shirekan sank his teeth into Terresca's leg, drawing blood and howls of pain from the stricken dragon. Alisia took advantage of the opportunity and hurled a number of lightning bolts, fireballs, and a huge ball of ice at the fallen beast. Terresca—not being able to move due to the pain and Shirekan's weight still upon him—created a magic shield of his own. Then with all his strength, he was able to throw Shirekan across the room, right into the unsuspecting Alisia, throwing both of them against the wall.

Valerian jumped to his feet and threw an onslaught of fireballs, lightning bolts, and ice spears. Then, using his magic ring, he took the form of a giant eagle, flew up and over to the pain-stricken dragon, and sank his talons into its back, again causing the dragon to howl in pain. Terresca, using his tail, batted Valerian back across the room, landing him next to Alisia and Shirekan. With the impact, Valerian was returned to his human form. After a few moments, Alisia and Valerian noticed no movement from Terresca.

"Do you think we've killed him?" Valerian asked.

Alisia, looking at her brother, said, "Well, he isn't moving. But maybe one of us should check."

Valerian—being the brave, strong man that he is—said, "Ladies first." He chuckled.

Just then, the mighty dragon rose to its feet and said, "Silly children, you are as dumb and ignorant as your mother before you."

Suddenly, hearing the word "mother" reminded Valerian of the image they had seen on the second night and the warning it gave them.

Turning to his sister, he said, "Alisia, the image—remember what it said?"

Alisia then said, "Of course. In order to defeat our enemy, we must strike at that which is empty."

Valerian then said, "What does it mean?"

Alisia then said, "I don't know, but we need time to figure it out." Then she added, "Shirekan, distract him while we think."

With this, the large cat leapt across the room. Landing on Terresca's back, he started digging in his claws. Terresca then started thrashing about, trying to shake the mighty cat loose.

"Clearly, the image is telling us to attack something that is empty—but what harm could be done by something empty?" Valerian said.

"Perhaps it's something on him that is empty?" Alisia responded.

Valerian then said, "Something empty on him?" After a pause, Valerian snapped his fingers and said, "That has to be it."

"What, what?" Alisia said.

The only part of that evil thing that is empty," Valerian responded, "is his heart!"

Alisia said, "Of course. But we'll have to attack together with all the power we can summon."

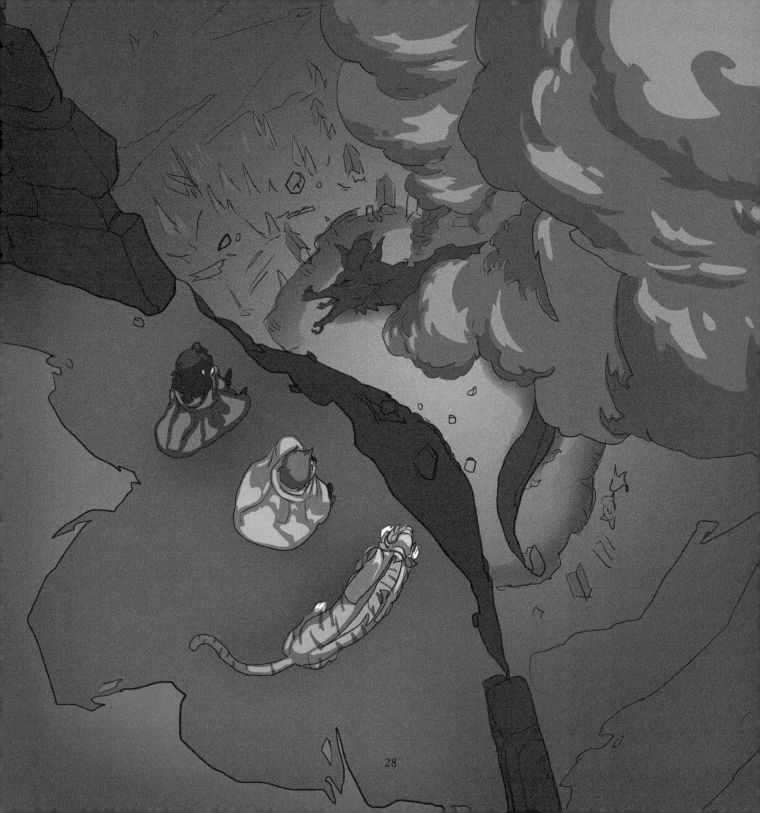

Just then, a loud haunting cry came from Terresca. Shirekan had dug his claws in so deep that the blood was gushing out in bucketfuls. As Terresca arched his back in pain, Shirekan leapt to the floor. Seizing their moment, Valerian and Alisia, joined hands and aimed towards the evil beast's heart. They attacked with the largest lightning bolt ever to be seen. The lightning bolt pierced Terresca's heart, going right through him and hitting the wall behind him. The result was a great explosion that knocked a huge hole in the side of the tower, through which Terresca's body was hurled.

All was quiet in Terresca's chamber, as the three walked slowly over to the hole. Looking through the hole, they saw Terresca's lifeless body lying on top of some rubble at the foot of the tower. As they watched, they saw a spark on Terresca's belly. Suddenly, Terresca's whole body was consumed by flames; and in an instant, there was nothing left but the ashes of the beast that once terrorized the land.

"Terresca is no more!" said a voice behind them.

Startled, they turned around to see Mordimar standing behind them.

"You have done well, my children. With Terresca's death, his evil reign is no more, and his magic is fading. Even now, the black cloud is lifting from Alestria. And as you can see outside, Terresca's troops are deserting his black tower."

Sure enough, they could see Terresca's minions fleeing from the tower. But even more amazing, they could see—for the first time in many, many years—a sunrise over Darkoria. Puzzled, they turned to Mordimar.

"Yes, children," he said. "Even Darkoria is no longer as dark as it once was, for Terresca used his magic to block the sun from Darkoria during his reign."

"Mordimar," Alisia asked, "was it you who was responsible for Terresca's magic mirror breaking and the report of us on the fifth level?"

"Yes," Mordimar replied.

"But if you could use your magic, why didn't you escape?" Valerian asked.

"Because," Mordimar explained, "Terresca put an anti-magic spell around my cell. Whenever I tried to use my magic, it would cancel it out. However, it didn't stop the two of you, because Terresca—assuming that since all thought I was dead, there would be no attempt to rescue me—only put the spell on magic coming from inside the cell. Since you were outside, your spells could work. And by opening my cell, you broke the spell, allowing me to use my magic freely again."

With this, the four of them, turned and went back into the chamber, whereupon Alisia and Valerian changed Shirekan back to his old self. With that accomplished, they began their preparations to leave for home. Finding a horse in the tower's stable for Mordimar, they went back down the hill to the little glen where they hid their horses and supplies. Mounting up, they turned toward the west, and began the trip back to Alestria.

The trip west was uneventful. With Terresca gone, the evil creatures of Darkoria had gone into hiding; and at any rate, they would not attack a group with a powerful wizard (not to mention some powerful young sorcerers) in it. Leaving Darkoria, they climbed back into the mountains. As they passed through to the other side, they could see that the cloud had indeed disappeared, and all of the western kingdoms were looking more beautiful than ever.

Upon reaching the borders of Alestria, the small company found that word of their deeds had come before them. Everywhere they went, grateful villagers would come out to greet then and give them gifts. As they traveled, they saw that their beautiful homeland had recovered from the ravages of the black cloud very well. One could not see any traces of the damage it caused; and if possible, Alestria looked even better than before.

Upon their arrival at the royal palace, they found their father waiting for them with open arms, and a huge welcome-back feast. Old King Vladimir's joy at his children's safe return, turned to shock when he saw the old wizard. "Mordimar? But how can this be? You're dead," said the king.

"In that there lies a tale, my old friend." Mordimar chuckled. "And I will share it with you while we enjoy this wonderful feast I see you've prepared."

So they went into the banquet hall, and the celebrations lasted long into the night. The next morning, as Mordimar was preparing to leave, he was interrupted by Vladimir and the twins.

"Mordimar, where are you going?" Alisia said.

"Alisia, my dear child, it is time for me to go back to where I came from," Mordimar answered.

Valerian then said, "But, Mordimar, your castle is no more. Terresca destroyed it during his rampages many years ago. And we had hopes that you would stay with us."

Mordimar replied, "You have no need for me here, for you two have conquered your greatest challenge, and you have nothing more to learn from me."

"Mordimar," King Vladimir said, "I feel I have known you my whole life, for my beautiful Rena thought of you as a father, and I know she would never have forgiven me if I did not insist upon you staying here with us. But to make it more appealing to you, I shall give you the old royal palace which my parents lived in until this palace was built."

"If my staying is that important to all of you, then it will be my pleasure to grant your wish," Mordimar replied.

So Mordimar took up residence in his new castle while Valerian and Alisia returned to their normal daily activities, and all was peaceful in Alestria once more. But every once in a while, Valerian and Alisia would feel a chill as if something evil was watching them, or a sinister laugh would be heard on the wind. And, though all said it was merely their imaginations, they couldn't help wondering if maybe it was . . . No, it couldn't be!

Or could it?

CPSIA information can be obtained
at www.ICGtesting.com
Printed in the USA
LVHW07s1420180518
577619LV00011B/25/P